MR ROUSE
BUILDS
HIS HOUSE

MR ROUSE BUILDS HIS HOUSE

By Stefan Themerson

English version by Stefan Themerson
and Barbara Wright

Drawings by Franciszka Themerson

Tate Publishing

First published in Polish by Mathesis Polska, Warsaw 1938
First published in English by Gaberbocchus Press, London 1950

This edition published 2013 by order of the Tate Trustees
by Tate Publishing, a division of Tate Enterprises Ltd,
Millbank, London SW1P 4RG
www.tate.org.uk/publishing

A catalogue record for this book is available from the British Library
ISBN 978-1-84976-154-3
Distributed in the United States and Canada by ABRAMS, New York
Library of Congress Control Number applied for

Reproduction by Evergreen Colour Separation Co. Ltd, Hong Kong
Printed in China by Toppan Leefung Printing Ltd

MIX
Paper from
responsible sources
FSC® C104723
FSC
www.fsc.org

CONTENTS :

BOOK I

MR ROUSE
BUILDS
HIS HOUSE

One day Mr Thomas Rouse went
to Mr Hilary Builder, the Architect,
and said:
        'Mr Builder,
        A.R.I.B.A.,
        I want to build a
        house, if I may?'

9

'What kind of house do you want?'

'Hm ... just an ordinary house,
    To eat in
    and sleep in –
    just like any other house.'

'Why of course, but all the same,' said Mr Builder standing up, 'there are houses and houses,
    and houses and houses,
    and houses and houses,
    and houses and houses,'

and he took a big book of drawings from his shelf. He dusted it and he
10   opened it.

'This is the house that the snail
     has grown,
   there's not much room in it,
   but it *is* his own,'

said Mr Hilary Builder, the Architect.   11

Mr Tom put on his glasses, looked carefully and said:

'I don't want to carry my house on my shoulders.'

'You're right,' said Mr Builder,
and he took out the second drawing.

'Mrs Owl lives in this hollow tree.'

'It may be alright for her,'
said Mr Tom,
'but it's certainly too owlish for me!'   13

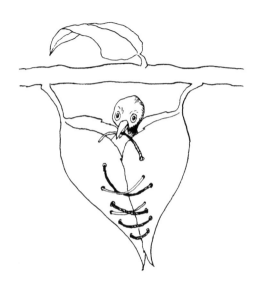

'The tailor-bird in India
stitches leaves together,
and sews a lovely villa
for him and his tail-feather.'

'But, Mr Builder, I'm not a bird, you know; how could I live in a house made of leaves?' asked Mr Tom.

'This underground flat
has been built by a mole.'

'He may call is that –
I'd call it a Hole!'
16   Said Mr Thomas Rouse firmly.

17

'The people who live in this house are from Togo,' said Mr Builder.

'But it's got no chimneys or windows!' said Mr Rouse angrily.

'Some Filipinos make
cottages on stakes.'

20

'This high house in Chinese is called PAGODA

Please!' 21

'Admire
  this cottage,
    it's covered with thatch.'

22

'And the thatch
may catch
fire,
And I'd rather have one
A little bit higher,'

said Mr Tom, 'so that even though
I haven't much land I can have more
rooms, and I don't want a wooden
house, but one made of brick, iron
or steel.'

23

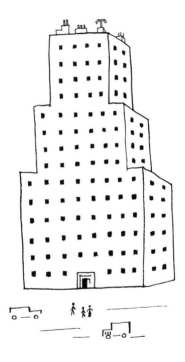

24

'This house
in New York
has been built
very high.
You can walk
up and walk
up and walk
to the sky.'

'You could ride up in a lift, I
suppose,' said Mr Thomas Rouse,
'but well, really, it's a bit too high
for me.'

'You are very difficult, Mr
Thomas Rouse,' said Mr Builder
the Architect, and he pulled still
another drawing out of his book.　25

Here it is:

'Flats next to flats;
 under flats, flats;
 and on top of these flats,
 more flats next to flats.'

'Oh, they're choking, they're choking!' exclaimed Mr Thomas Rouse.

'What's the matter? Who's choking?'

'The houses!
The houses
are choking!
They're jammed
so close together
that I wouldn't be surprise
if one of them SCREAMED!'

'I must have a little house with a garden that has flower beds and a little bench. And the house must have large windows with window boxes. And in the window boxes and on the balcony there must be flowers.'

'Very well,' said Mr Builder, 'I'll draw you a house like that. With flowers.'

'Don't want it on paper,'
			said Mr Tom Rouse,
'I want you to build me,
	to BUILD me a house!'

'Of course, Mr Rouse, but
first I think what you want, then I
draw what I think, and then I
build what I draw!'

Mr Builder
A.R.I.B.A.
is working at his drawing board
early in the day.

First
he
does some thinking
in his head
in his big head.

Then
he draws
some lines in ink in
black
blue
green
and
30   red.

Then
he makes
some calculations,
crosses them out
And makes them again:
How
deep
to build the
foundations
so that they'll stand the house's strain.

Then he does
some arithmetic
to find
how thick
the wall will be
if it isn't just ONE brick thick
but
   THREE.

Dring dring ...

Telephone!

'Hallo!
Is that Mr Rouse?
This is Mr Builder the Architect;
Plans
okay
we'll start the building
right away.'

'Hooray!'

BOOK II

MR ROUSE
GOES TO SEE
HIS HOUSE

'Hooray!' exclaimed Mr Tom Rouse, 'I want to see how you build a house. I'll be there in a minute.'

'And where are you? – very far away?'

'The other side of the wood and the other side of the river.'

'Then you'd better hurry!'

'I *am* hurrying,' said Mr Tom, and he tried to climb into the telephone receiver.

But he couldn't get in, because he
was too big and the receiver was too
38 small.

So he exclaimed:

'I can't travel by phone because I'm too big and the phone's too small.'

'Ha! ha! ha!' laughed Mr Builder. 'Of course you can't. Only a word can travel by phone.
Even the longest one.
Even one like this: LLANFAIRPWLLG-WYNGYLLGOGERYCHWYRNDROBBWLLLLANTSILIO-GOGOGOCH.'

'LLANFAIRPWLLGWYNGYLLGOGERYCHWYRND-ROBBWLLLLANTSILIOGOGOGOCH!' repeated Mr Tom.

'But a man, even the smallest one, even one smaller than the small–est mosquito, doesn't know how to travel by phone.'

'In that case,' said Mr Tom, 'I'd better put on my galoshes and come quickly on foot.'

'You'd better t...' exclaimed Mr Builder, but Mr Tom wasn't listening any longer. He hung up the receiver and rushed out into the street.

He walked and walked:

on Monday
    he walked along the Broadway
on Tuesday
    he walked along a high-way
on Wednesday
    he walked along a roadway
on Thursday
    he walked along a causeway
on Friday
    he walked along a byway
on Saturday
    he walked along a pathway
on Sunday
    he walked across some fields.

And in the middle of the field there
was a box. It was a telephone box.   41

So Mr Tom went into the box and put two pennies in the slot, and when he heard the dialling tone, he dialled this number:

111555

because that was Mr Hilary Builder's telephone number.

'Hallo! Is that Mr Builder? This is Tom Rouse. I've been walking and walking and walking and walking ...'

'And we've been working and working and working and working,' said Mr Builder, 'and we've already laid the foundations. You'll have to be quicker than that!'

'All right, I'll take a cab.'

'You'd better take ...' exclaim-ed Mr Builder, but Mr Tom wasn't listening any longer. He hung up the receiver, rushed out of the tele-phone box into the road and shouted: 'Cab!'

And a cab came out of the forest. Mr Tom jumped into it and they drove off.

They drove and they drove.

The first day the driver sat back comfortably on his seat, held the reins and sang:

'I am a merry cabman,
a cab – *Giddy up!* – man
I've been driving round in this old
crate since the story first began.
44   *Giddy up!*'

And the horse beat time with his hooves:

'a-clip, a-clop,
a-clippety-clop.'

45

The second day the cabman cracked his whip and sang:

'I am a merry driver, see how
        cleverly I drive;
I don't say I'll get you there today,
        but you're certain to arrive –
Some day.'

And the horse beat time with his hooves:

        'a-clip,
        a-clop,
        a-clippety-clop.'

    And the third day the cab driver heaved a sigh and sang:

'I am a merry charioteer,
Oh what a life, oh dear,
     oh dear!'

'What are you grumbling about?' Mr Tom asked.

'Why shouldn't I grumble?' said the driver, 'when nowadays everybody is in such a hurry that they don't want to hire cabs.'

'Oh, I'm in a hurry too,' said Mr Tom.

'Well in that case you'd better go by bus,' said the cab driver, and he drove Mr Tom to the bus stop.

And there, near the bus stop, was a telephone box.

Mr Tom went into the box, put in two pennies, took the receiver off and dialled this number:

111555

'Hallo! Is that Mr Builder? How's my house, please?'

'The walls are two storeys high, do try to hurry!'

'I'll try. I'll come by bus.'

'You'd better take an ...' ex–claimed Mr Builder, but Tom Rouse wasn't listening any longer. He hung up the receiver, rushed out of the telephone box and jumped into a bus.

'Grrr ...' growled the bus, and started off.

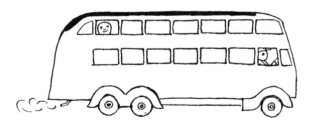

It drove all day.

And Mr Tom looked out of the window.

And thought:
   'If they're already up to the second floor, I really am late.'

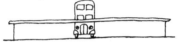

And then suddenly: HALT! They had come to a level crossing and the gates were closed. The train was coming.

But Mr Tom felt he simply couldn't wait until the road was clear. He jumped out of the bus and rushed to the telephone in the station.

'This is me again,
  I really am hurrying ...'

'Good,
  we're putting on the roof
  and I wanted to explain ...'

'Oof!
  I'll take a train,
  it's coming now, choof choof ...'

'I wanted to explain that you'd
better take an aero...' shouted
Mr Builder, but Mr Tom wasn't
listening any longer. He hung up
the receiver, rushed out onto the
platform and jumped onto the train. 51

But suddenly he heard:
    COCKADOODLEDOO!

He turned to what it was, but then from behind him he heard:
    GA! GA! GA!

Mr Tom didn't like it, and he jumped out of the train.

And at that moment the engine grunted and the train moved off.

'Wait for me! Wait for me! Wait for me!' shouted Mr Tom.

But the train was shouting something else. Something like this:

'You're *far* too slow! You're *far* too slow! You're *far* too slow!'

And it escaped.

Off rushed Mr Tom to the telephone.

'Hallo! Is that Mr Builder? I'm ringing you again from the same place. The train ran away from me.'

'Really, Mr Tom,' said Mr Builder,
  'Can't you come any faster?
  The walls have been covered
    with plaster,
  The glaziers have been –
  the glass they put in the win-
    dows is lovely and clean,
  and the sun is gleaming in it.
  The painters have finished just
    this minute,
  The lockmakers are putting the
    locks on the doors,
  And the parquet-floor layers are
    laying the floors.'

'Oh, dear, oh dear,
  I'm not even very near ...'

'Then you'd better take an aero–
plane!' exclaimed Mr Builder.

'Why on earth didn't you sug–
gest that at first?'

'I DID' answered Mr Build–
er, but Mr Tom wasn't listening
any more. He had put down the
receiver and was rushing to the aero–
drome.

He jumped into a plane and flew
off.

Frrr ... Wrrr ... and he had
arrived over the house.

He looked down, and where there had been an empty space before, there was now a big house. Exactly the same as Mr Architect Hilary Builder had drawn on paper.

Mr Tom looked down and shouted:

'Hooray! Hooray for every–thing!'

'Hooray! Hooray for every–
thing!' he repeated, opened his
umbrella and flew down to the
ground.

BOOK III

MR ROUSE
GOES OVER
HIS HOUSE

Said Mr Tom Rouse:

'I should like to go over my house.'

'All right,' said Mr Builder, taking Mr Tom's arm, 'come on.'

So they went.

'This is the gate,' explained Mr Builder, 'it has an electric lock. When you hear your friends knock you don't need to rush out into the street, and they don't need to wait. You just press a button in the house, and the gate opens by itself.'

'That's clever,' said Mr Tom appreciatively.

'There'll be a little garden here, and behind the house there'll be an orchard.'

'And will you build real cherry trees in the orchard?' asked Mr Tom, and he looked admiringly at

Mr Architect.

'And how do you get into the house?'

'Through this door;
the key sticks a bit,
and the hinges
scream from time to time;
you have to oil them with spit
or, better still, with oil,
(but that doesn't rhyme).'

'I'll remember to do that,' said Mr Tom, and he opened the door. Behind the door was the staircase.

63

MR TOM VISITS
THE STAIRCASE

By the banisters
the stairs knelt,
and quarrelled –

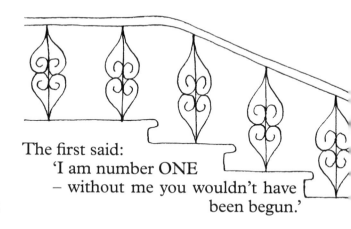

The first said:
'I am number ONE
– without me you wouldn't have
been begun.'

The second said:
    'Well I am TWO,
       so I'm a better stair than you.'

The third said:
    'Huh! I'm number THREE;
    you could even fall down–
         stairs from me.'

The fourth said:
    'FOUR, let *me* tell *you*,
    is THREE plus ONE,
    or TWO times TWO.'

The   fifth   said: 'FIVE',
the   sixth   said: 'SIX';
the   seventh   said: 'STOP
              talking politics –'

Just at that moment Mr Tom
came into the house.

He didn't wait till they had
finished their discussion,

first stair,
the
he stepped on

66

                                                    seventh stair,

                                              the

                                  sixth stair,

                            the

                      fifth stair,

                  the

            fourth stair,

        the

      third stair,

  the

second stair,

the

and   rushed   up   to   the   attic.   67

MR TOM VISITS THE ROOF

The roof is covered with slates
and almost anything irritates these
    slates.
When the chimney sweep skates
    on them
they growl:
'Take care!'
And when a burglar skulks about
    on them
(because that does sometimes
    happen too),
they glare
and call out: 'Get down, you
    owl!'

That's the sort of slates they are –
Bossy.

All round the roof runs the gutter,
very dapper
and greedy;
it drinks up all the water from the
            rain
splutter splutter.
'Glup ... glup ... glup,'
it yells,
and compels
the water to run down to the
            drain.

MR TOM VISITS
THE CHIMNEYS

And he sees
the chimneys
insolently pulling faces.

'And what would happen if we
stopped letting the smoke out?'
they asked.

'What would happen?
I'd call a chimney sweep,
He'd wipe your dirty noses for
    you!

A chimney sweep to a flue
is like castor oil to me or you!'

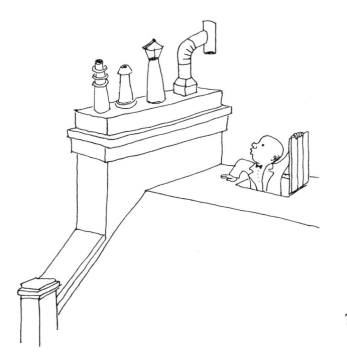

MR TOM LOOKS AT THE SKY

It can rain if it likes;
it can snow
if it particularly wants to,
but Mr Tom can look at the sky
and still keep dry.
How?

Through the window!

MR TOM GOES OUT ON THE BALCONY

The red geraniums were talking
to the chestnut tree very impudently:

'We're taller than you,
  so boo!
  Although we only grow in flower
      pots
  we look down on you.
  Oh look, there are lots
  of caterpillars walking on top of
      your green head!'
  That's the sort of thing they
      said,
  the geraniums that grew on the
      balcony.

MR TOM JUMPS FOR JOY

'Oh, Mr Builder, you *are* a
clever man!'
exclaimed Mr Tom,

'Everything is just as beautiful
as it was in your plan.'

and he threw his arms round him
and kissed him.

And then he hugged the mason

who had built the walls

And the painter

who had painted the house

And the glazier

who had put the glass
in the windows

And the chimney sweep,
who had climbed up to the roof,
Mr Tom
couldn't stop
hugging
him –

OOF!

BOOK IV

MR ROUSE
TURNS ON
THE TAP

Mr Tom Rouse went to see
Mr Waterspout,
but Mr Waterspout
was out
playing cricket in the street.

82

Mr Tom Rouse waited politely on the pavement and watched the game, as he didn't want to be a nuisance.

And only when the ball fell into a water butt did he say:
'I am Tom Rouse,
I've built a house,
but in this house there isn't any water.'

'Oh dear,' said Mr Waterspout sympathetically. 'Come to my office and we'll find something to help you.'

The gentlemen went into a big room which was Mr Waterspout's office. Mr Tom sat down at one side of the desk and Mr Water-spout sat down at the other side of the desk and called:

'Ginger!'

'Yes sir ...'

'Will you show Mr Tom Rouse our FIRST CONTRAPTION.'

Ginger poked about in the corner where the spiders lived and picked up this:

Mr Tom got up from his arm-chair. Ginger put THIS,

or THE FIRST CONTRAPTION
on his shoulders.

At the end of the ropes he fixed
two buckets.

'This is called a yoke,' said Mr
Waterspout. 'You carry it down to
the river and bring back the water
with it.'

'Pooh!' scoffed Mr Tom Rouse
'I don't think much of that idea!'

'You needn't get so cross,' said Mr Waterspout, 'it was a very useful invention once upon a time. However if it doesn't suit you we'll try and find something else. Here's THE SECOND CONTRAPTION.

Ding dong bell!
We can dig a well
and pull up water in buckets from
the well for Mrs and Mr Tom.

People always used to get water like that.'

'Hm,' said Mr Tom, 'they *used* to. But they don't now.

And to do all that you have to be strong.
And I'm not strong.

And to do all that you need plenty of time.
And I haven't got plenty of time.

And my son Josh
would rather not wash!'

So then Mr Waterspout showed
Mr Tom this:

THE THIRD CONTRAPTION

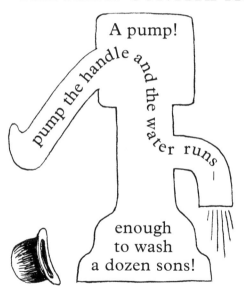

A pump!

pump the handle and the water runs

enough
to wash
a dozen sons!

'But how –' exclaimed Mr Tom Rouse, 'but how shall I carry the water up to the first floor to the sec**ond...** *second floor to the third floor to...'*

That's an awful lot of water. If I want everyone in the house to have enough I shall have to be carrying it upstairs all day.'

'Oh,' said Mr Waterspout, 'then we'll put pipes in your house, and the water will flow up through those pipes to the first floor to the sec**ond**

'Now that begins to sound in–teresting, said Mr Tom. 'But who will pump up such a lot of water every day?'

'On top of a hill
there's a great big tower
where they pump the town's water
90   by electric power.

To that water tower
I'll connect your house.
What do you think of that,
Mr Thomas Rouse?'

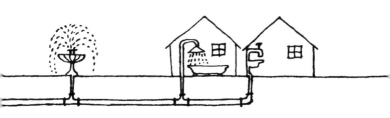

Mr Tom Rouse shook hands with
Mr Waterspout and said:
    'That sounds a very fine contrap–
tion, and I'm not worried any more.' 91

The workmen arrived
and contrived
to dig
a great big
ditch
along the street, in which
to install the pipes.

BOYNG!

And then they came
to do the same
in the basement, to bore
a hole in the floor
to install the pipes.

BOYNG!

Then work was begun
so the pipes could run
and the water could flow
from the main below
to the very top of the house.

BOYNG!

They worked all night –
quite right!

They put in the taps,
Chaps!

93

And the bath tub –

you Grub!

And the hand basin to wash

the dirty hands of Josh.

And the kitchen sink –

so I should think!

And they were not at all shy
when they came to supply
something else very
necessary –

What?

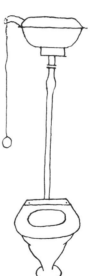

Underneath the pavement
there are other pipes too
for taking dirty water
away.

Away from your house,
and away from Mr Tom's house
it flows, unseen,
away.

Dirty chap –
get those hands under the tap!

BOOK V

MR ROUSE
SWITCHES ON
THE LIGHT

Mr Tom Rouse went shuffling along Dark Street, zig zag, zig zag.

And he went scritch scratch with his walking stick, so as not to bump into anyone; so as not to crash into anyone.

Because in Dark Street it was absolutely dark.

☞ In this picture there are houses on both sides of the street, and Mr Tom is walking along in between the houses.

If it weren't so dark you could see all that very easily.

In Light Street it was, of course, very light, and just at the corner where Light and Dark streets met, there was a shop.

Over the entrance shone these letters:

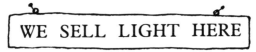

WE SELL LIGHT HERE

Mr Tom went in and said:

'I should like to buy some light.'

'Certainly, Sir,' said the Assistant, 'Come this way, Sir,' said the Assistant

(who was terribly polite).

And he led Mr Tom to a show case with a glass window. And in this show case there was a plant in a flower pot. And on one leaf of the plant that was in the flower pot something was shining in the dark. Mr Tom put on his glasses and looked carefully.

And the Assistant said:

'This is a glow worm;
    it's the speciality of our well-
        known firm.
Do you wish me to wrap it for you, Sir?'

'Oh, what an idea!' said Mr Tom indignantly.

'Then perhaps this will suit you better, Sir?

It's phosphorescent the tail end,
It's luminous the head end,
It's fished from the bottom of
    the ocean,
And it swims in perpetual
    motion!'

Mr Tom looked with interest at the phosphorescent fish swimming in the aquarium, but he shook his head and said:

'No; that won't suit me any better.'

Then the Assistant led Mr Rouse
up to a little room which had no

ceiling at all. And no roof. And
overhead you could see the sky, and
in the sky you could see the stars
and the moon.

'Now that light up there,' said
the Assistant, 'just to do you a
favour, I can let you have at a ridicul-
ously low price; but you'll have to
take it with you.'

'I'll try,' said Mr Tom Rouse.

So he put a table in the middle of the room,
he put a wardrobe on the table,
  and a stool on the wardrobe,
  and a chair on the stool,
  and a little stool on the chair,
  and he climbed up onto the little
                                    stool.
  He   stood   on   tiptoes,   and   he
stretched out his arms ...

But it was still much
much
much
much
much
much
much
much
much
much
much
much
much too far
to the moon.

'Well in that case we must look for something else,' said the Assistant, and he showed Mr Tom this:

'This magnificent torch
hangs up by the porch ...'

'But it smokes, and blackens everything near it, and anyway I want the light in the rooms, not by the porch,' retorted Mr Tom.
'Take it away!'

'If that doesn't suit you, if you would like to come here ...'

Mr Tom went there ... and suddenly exclaimed:

'Oh help! Mother!
Not candles, no fear!
They drop wax in my ear!'

and he escaped.

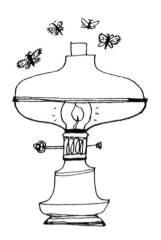

'And oil lamps make
my eyes ache.

What I want is …'

'What?'

'THIS!'

'The filament inside this bulb becomes white-hot and shines.'

'And what makes it white-hot?'

'Current.'

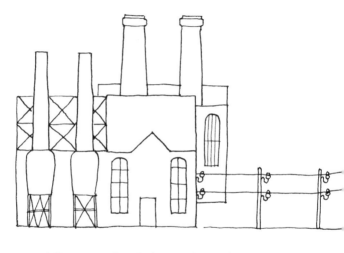

'Current?   Where from?'

'From here, Mr Tom!

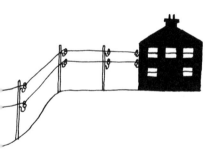

To this power station
I'll connect your house;
What d'you think of that,
Mr Thomas Rouse?'

The workmen arrived
and contrived
to dig
a great big
ditch
along the street, in which
to lay the cables.

HEAVE!

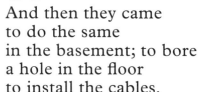

And then they came
to do the same
in the basement; to bore
a hole in the floor
to install the cables.

PHEW!

Then work was begun
so the wires could run
from the cable below,
and the current could flow
to every bulb in the house.

SWISH!

Look, here's a small
hole in the wall.
In the wall is a hole,
in the hole is a little tube,
and in the tube, two wires
in their jerseys.

In their jerseys!
Whatever for?

So that the current doesn't escape
  from the wires.
You don't know what that's called
  I expect.

I do – INSULATION!

Correct.

116   Here's the watt-meter,

Here's the water-heater.

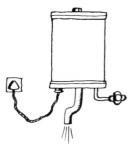

This is the wall-socket –
don't knock it!

Here's the plug,
and here's the switch.
Which is which?

Here's a mirror light,
very bright.

And here's a hook.

Look,

the lamp will hang from it.   119

There's an electric bell
as well.'

 Even the iron
has a wire on

And
there's
te-
le-
vi-
si-
on!

BOOK VI

MR ROUSE
WAKES UP EARLY

Mr Tom slept very soundly. And
then he woke up and wondered:
WHAT'S THE TIME?

He looked at his grandfather's portrait on the wall.

But the face of the portrait didn't show
THE TIME.

He took a little round box of peppermints out of his pocket.

But the lid of the little round box of peppermints didn't show
THE TIME.

So Mr Tom got up.

He washed and he dressed and he went out into the street.

He went to a café, but the café was closed.

On the door was a padlock, and a notice:

GOOD BREAKFASTS SERVED
HERE
open at 8 a.m.

'It must be too early,' thought Mr Tom, and he went home again.

He made his bed, swept the floor dusted the lampshade, ironed his handkerchiefs, and went out into the garden. In the garden he hoed the flower-beds and watered the flowers, and then he washed his hands and went out into the street again.

And in the sky the moon was shining and the stars were twinkling

Off went Mr Tom to the café once more.

But the café was closed.

On the door was a padlock, and a notice:

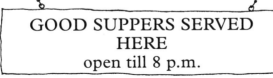

GOOD SUPPERS SERVED
HERE
open till 8 p.m.

'Oh dear,' thought Mr Tom.
And he went away.

But he didn't go home.

He walked and he walked and he
walked and he walked until he came
to the street that was called:

MASTER CLOCKMAKER'S STREET

He went to the first clockmaker and said:

'I am Tom Rouse and I have built a house. But in this house there is not a single clock, and so I'm always either too late or too early.'

'Oh! That's too bad!' said the clockmaker. 'But you've come to the right man. I happen to be the inventor of the first clock in the world.'

THE FIRST CLOCKMAKER'S CLOCK

'My clock is just made of sun
and shadow.

If you ask yourself in the morning:
  'What's the time?'
the answer might be:
  'the big shadow of the chimney
    is just on the spinney.'

      And at midday
      the shadow is short –
      it's not quite up to the
                tennis court.'

'And where is the shadow at night?' asked Mr Tom.

'At night? Nothing doing! You'll have to wait till it's light!'

'Oh dear, I'm awfully sorry,' said Mr Tom, 'but I'm looking for a clock that can tell me the time at night as well.'

That's what he said, and he bowed and went away. And he went to the second clockmaker.

THE SECOND
CLOCKMAKER'S CLOCK

'You take a huge bowl of water,
at the bottom make a hole;
and then you let the water drip
into the other bowl.'

'That's a very funny clock,' said Mr Tom. 'And what time does it say now?'

The clockmaker looked carefully at the two bowls and said:

'A quarter of a bowl past dinner!'

'Huh!' said Mr Tom Rouse, 'But when do you have your dinner?'

That's what Mr Tom said, and he went on his way down Master Clockmaker's Street.

THE THIRD
CLOCKMAKER'S CLOCK

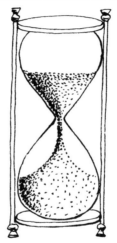

This is what the third clockmaker had to say about his clock:

'A very short time
equals one grain of sand;
for it all to run through
will take much longer, and

then the clock must be turned
upside down, so the sand
can start over again
running through the clock, and

then the clock must be turned
upside down, so the sand ...'

'Yes, yes,' exclaimed Mr Tom,
'I understand. My Granny had a
clock exactly like that. She always
used it when she boiled eggs.'

THE FOURTH
CLOCKMAKER'S CLOCK

The fourth clockmaker said:

'A salient feature
of my candle clock
is its silent movement –
no tick-tock.'

'And how do you find out what the time is?' asked Mr Tom.

'On the candle are notches;
the flame will devour
the wax between each
in exactly one hour.'

'That's a very nice clock,' said Mr Tom, 'but it would be too much trouble, and it wouldn't be accurate enough.'

That's what Mr Tom said; but he also said, 'Good-bye.'

And he went away.

To the fifth clockmaker.

THE FIFTH
CLOCKMAKER'S CLOCK

The fifth clockmaker lived in a very high tower.

'Could you please sell me a clock?' asked Mr Tom.

'With pleasure,' replied the clockmaker. 'If you like I'll take you in.'

And they went into the clock.

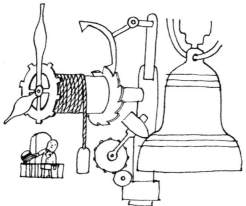

Huge weights pull the rope
and the rope turns the wheels;
huge hands show the time
and the huge bell peals:

BIM BAM BOOM

and the pendulum ticks:

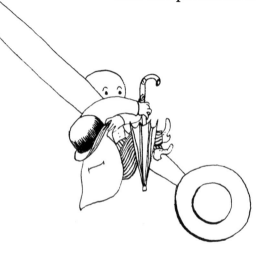

TICK   TOCK

and the clockmaker says:

'That's THE clock.'

'But it's miles too big for my room,' yelled Mr Tom, and he jumped out onto the stairs and escaped.

THE SIXTH
CLOCKMAKER'S CLOCK

Mr Tom went to the sixth clock–maker and said:

'I am Tom Rouse and I have built a house. But in this house there is not a single clock, and so you see I never know

THE TIME.'

'Oh! We'll soon put that right,' said the clockmaker, and he showed Mr Tom a hundred-and-fifty clocks

and watches.

Clocks that hung on the wall,
large and small;

and watches to fix on your wrist
(wrist-watches);

and the kind with a bell,
to wake you up in the morning,
(alarm clocks).

And he said:

'If you want to know the hour
just look at the little hand;
   that's all.

And if you want to know how
many minutes past the hour it is
you just look at the big hand;
that's all.'

Mr Tom liked all those very much, and so he bought himself

one clock, to hang on the wall;

one wrist-watch, to fix on his wrist;

one alarm clock, to wake him up in the morning.

THE END OF THE
ADVENTURES OF
MR ROUSE